First published 1993 in Great Britain by Hamish Hamilton Ltd

First U.S. edition 1994

Cataloging-in-Publication Data available upon request.

ISBN 0-15-200549-8

Printed in Hong Kong

A B C D E

ANN TURNBULL

Too Tired

Illustrated by Emma Chichester Clark

Gulliver Books
Harcourt Brace & Company
San Diego   New York   London

"Hurry! Hurry!"
The flood was coming.

All the animals climbed aboard the Ark: lions and lizards, tigers and tree frogs, kangaroos and kinkajous; two of every animal under the sun.

Down came the rain. The waters rose.
The flood rolled over the earth.

Noah checked his list:
"Goats?"
"*Meh.*"
"Owls?"
"*Whoo-oo.*"
"Sloths? . . . Sloths?"
"No sloths," said Shem.
"They don't want to come," said Ham.
"Too tired," said Japhet.
"Too tired!" said Noah. "They must come.
They are on the list."

Deep in the rain forest, under the green whistling canopy of leaves, two sloths slept. They were tired. They were always tired. They hung as still as the moss growing on the trees, as still as the leaf mold under the flood.

All around them the forest was stirring. Spider monkeys leapt from tree to tree, eager to reach the Ark; macaws shouted; bellbirds called. But the sloths didn't hear them.

Rain roared in the treetops. The flood was rising.
Parrots scolded, "Wake up! Wake up!"
The sloths slept.

Toucans shouted, "Wake up! Wake up!
The Ark is coming. You must get aboard."
Slowly the sloths woke and stretched.
"Tomorrow," they said.
"Today!" screeched the birds.
But the sloths had gone back to sleep.

The Ark came closer to the sloths' tree.
"Wake them up," said Noah. "Tell them they are on the list."
The lions roared.
The dogs barked.

The elephants trumpeted.
The sheep bleated.
The howler monkeys howled.
But the cats said, "Who cares? Let them drown."

The sloths woke and saw that the water was rising.
Slowly, slowly, they moved to a higher branch.
Slowly, slowly, they curled their claws around it.

"Jump!" shouted the animals. "Swim to the Ark!"
But the sloths had gone back to sleep.
The water was rising, rising up the tree trunk.
Soon it would reach the sloths.

"Swim!" roared the lions.
"Swim!" called the parrots.
"Swim!" barked the dogs.
Slowly the sloths woke once again. They considered the problem. They could swim but they preferred not to.
"Tomorrow," they said.
"Today!" shouted the animals.

The sloths' branch dipped and wobbled.
The water lapped at their fur.
"Who cares?" said the cats.
"We care," said the other animals. And they
roared and barked and trumpeted and bleated
and howled and screeched
to keep the sloths awake.

Ham brought the Ark in nearer. The dogs barked, "Save them!
Save them!" and rushed up and down the deck. Noah tapped
his list. "We can't leave them behind," he said.

The elephants had been thinking. They went to the side of the Ark. They hung their trunks over the side, but they couldn't quite reach the sloths. They leaned over again, stretching, stretching, stretching.

All the animals crowded to the side to watch. The Ark tilted. The elephants caught hold of the sloths. They pulled them off their branch and lifted them into the air and down onto the deck.

All the animals cheered, except the cats.
"Such a fuss," said the cats.

Noah checked his list again:
"Dogs?"
"*Ruff, ruff, ruff.*"
"Mice?"
"*Squeak.*"

"Sloths? . . . Sloths?"
The sloths hung from a pole on the deck.
Their wet fur steamed in the sun.
They were fast asleep.